NICKELODEON
THE BIG GREEN HELP™

WITHDRAWN

NICKELODEON
SPONGEBOB SQUAREPANTS

# SPONGEBOB TO THE RESCUE!

## A TRASHY TALE ABOUT RECYCLING

by Alison Inches
illustrated by Gibbs Rainock

 W9-CAJ-717

Simon Spotlight/
Nickelodeon
New York London
Toronto Sydney

*Stephen Hillenburg*

Based on the TV series *SpongeBob SquarePants*® created by Stephen Hillenburg as seen on Nickelodeon®

SIMON SPOTLIGHT

An imprint of Simon & Schuster Children's Publishing Division
1230 Avenue of the Americas, New York, New York 10020
© 2010 Viacom International Inc. All rights reserved. NICKELODEON, *SpongeBob SquarePants*,
and all related titles, logos, and characters are registered trademarks of Viacom International Inc. Created by Stephen Hillenburg.
All rights reserved, including the right of reproduction in whole or in part in any form.
SIMON SPOTLIGHT and colophon are registered trademarks of Simon & Schuster, Inc.
LITTLE GREEN BOOKS and associated colophon are trademarks of Simon & Schuster, Inc.
The Big Green Help, and all related titles, logos, and characters are trademarks of Viacom International Inc.
For information about special discounts for bulk purchases, please contact Simon & Schuster Special Sales
at 1-866-506-1949 or business@simonandschuster.com.
Manufactured in the United States of America 0210 LAK
First Edition    10 9 8 7 6 5 4 3 2 1
ISBN 978-1-4169-9592-0

3 8510 10172 6523

On the way home from work SpongeBob spied something by the side of the road. "Wow, an old propeller!" he exclaimed. "This will make a *great* lawn ornament! Hmm, I never realized how much neat stuff people leave lying around."
So SpongeBob picked up the propeller and headed home.

The next day SpongeBob brought home an old tire, a forgotten laundry basket, and a worn-out boot. Patrick and Gary stared at the pile of junk.

"This must be my lucky week!" SpongeBob told them. "I can turn this old tire into a swing and this laundry basket into a playpen for Gary."

"Meow," said Gary.

"Sorry, Gary," said SpongeBob. "Not a playpen—I meant luxury snail house."

"But, SpongeBob, it's just a bunch of junk!" Patrick exclaimed.

"Patrick, my friend," said SpongeBob, "you may see junk, but I see possibilities. Haven't you heard the old saying, 'One man's junk is another man's treasure'?"

"Ooh, is it a pirate treasure?" Patrick asked with newfound excitement.

Everywhere SpongeBob went he kept an eye out for junk. He checked the gutters. He looked in the storm drains. He combed the beach at Goo Lagoon. SpongeBob found everything from empty soda cans to plastic milk jugs.

"Hello there, ginormous clam!" said SpongeBob as he walked past. "Are you going to eat that bottle cap in your shell?"

The giant clam shook his head no, and SpongeBob plucked the cap out of his shell.

Then SpongeBob passed a dolphin tangled in an old fishing net.

"Hey, friend!" called SpongeBob. "May I have that net when you're done playing with it?"

The dolphin struggled this way and that as he tried to free himself.

"I'll take that as a yes!" said SpongeBob, and he untangled the dolphin.

"Thanks, pal," said the dolphin as he swam away.

"No, no! Thank *you*!" said SpongeBob. "This fishing net will make a perfect hammock for my backyard!"

Over the next week SpongeBob's junk collection grew and grew.

"Gee, Gary," said SpongeBob. "I better organize this stuff until I can make good use of it all. It's beginning to take over the house."

SpongeBob bought several bins, labeled them, and placed them outside his house.

"Junk, sweet junk!" sang SpongeBob as he organized. "The possibilities are endless. Junk can become art, or a place to sit, or a pretty decoration. . . ."

"Or a total EYESORE!" yelled Squidward, who had stopped to have a look.

"It's not an eyesore, it's my treasure!" SpongeBob replied. "Someday this junk will be worth something!"

"Worth something!" exclaimed Squidward, laughing. "Hmm, let me see. A pile of junk plus a pile of junk equals- that's right-a whole lot of JUNK!"

But SpongeBob paid no attention to Squidward. He was too busy making plans for his junk.

On Saturday, SpongeBob decided to take a break from organizing his junk collection to go jellyfishing with Patrick.

"I got one, Patrick!" shouted SpongeBob as he dropped his net on the creature.

"Uh, SpongeBob, I don't think that's a jellyfish," said Patrick. "It looks like a plastic bag."

"It *is* a plastic bag, Patrick!" SpongeBob said, almost as excited as if he'd caught an actual jellyfish. "This will be great for my collection! I can't believe I used to catch plastic bags and just throw them back. I can use this on my next shopping trip!"

"Wow," said Patrick. "I hope I catch a plastic bag. Sounds handy."

When SpongeBob got home from jellyfishing, he found his collection bins overflowing. Friends and neighbors had dropped off old hubcaps, flip-flops, toaster ovens, television sets, baby strollers, and some broken toys.

"These bins sure are a great idea, SpongeBob!" said a passerby as he tossed in an old vacuum cleaner.

SpongeBob was overwhelmed. It would take him a whole week to organize all of that new junk!

A few days later Mr. Krabs stopped by—but not to drop off junk.

"Lad, where ya been?" Mr. Krabs was panicked. "It's been days since you fried up a Krabby Patty! This junk collection is a great hobby, but you've got a heap o' hungry customers to feed, and I've got a pile o' money to start collectin'!"

"Don't worry, Mr. Krabs!" said SpongeBob. "I'm almost done organizing the new additions. I promise I'll report for duty right after I finish."

"I'll be expecting you," said Mr. Krabs. "On the double!"

But SpongeBob couldn't report to the Krusty Krab. His junk pile kept growing bigger and bigger until it was too big for his bins. He asked Sandy to help him replace them with supersize Dumpsters.

"Way to go, SpongeBob!" said Sandy. "This here recycling center is exactly what Bikini Bottom has always needed."

"What do you mean?" SpongeBob asked, confused. "*This* is a junk collection. What's recycling?"

"Recycling means separating leftover junk into bins—just like *you* did—and taking it to special processing centers where it can be made into something new! Recycling makes your surroundings look nice. It also saves sea critters from getting tangled in trash—or worse—mistaking trash for food, which can kill them."

SpongeBob's eyes grew big with horror. "You mean those sea creatures who shared their trash with me weren't playing with it?"

"I doubt it," said Sandy. "They were probably trying to get free."

Then a great light shined on SpongeBob.

"I *must* save Bikini Bottom from the perils of trash!" he declared.

So SpongeBob worked even harder. He collected more junk and trash, and sorted it day and night. By this point everyone in Bikini Bottom had heard about SpongeBob's recycling center. When the Dumpsters filled up, Sandy helped take them to the processing centers and then helped bring in new ones.

The harder SpongeBob worked, the more the trash piled up.
"You've got to slow down, little buddy," said Sandy. "This is
too much work for one little guy."

"But, Sandy, I'm doing this for Bikini Bottom!" replied
SpongeBob, frazzled.

Sandy started to worry. The next day she stopped into
the Krusty Krab to see SpongeBob only to find out that
he still hadn't come back to work. It had been two weeks!
Finally she decided it was time to pay a visit to her friends
at city hall and see if they could help.

SpongeBob continued to sort junk, but the junk was winning. Soon he found himself on top of a mountain of trash. He panted and sputtered. His eyelids and body drooped—even Squidward was worried.

"Look, SpongeBob," called Squidward from below. "Recycling is a good cause, but, uh, Mr. Krabs needs you, and I'm tired of doing all the work!"

SpongeBob just lay there with his eyes closed.

"SpongeBob?" called Squidward. "SpongeBob, quit joking around!"

But SpongeBob wasn't joking around. He was exhausted!

When he stirred, SpongeBob heard the roar of a crowd. He pinched himself.
"What's going on?" SpongeBob asked in a daze. "Am I a rock star?"
Sandy slapped SpongeBob on the back.
"No, little guy," said Sandy, laughing.
"Oh," said SpongeBob. "Then why is everyone in Bikini Bottom staring at us?"
"Turn around, SpongeBob," said Sandy. "You'll see!"

SpongeBob turned around and saw a building with his name on it. Inside there were three enormous Dumpsters, each with a different label: GLASS AND PLASTIC, ALUMINUM, and PAPER AND CARDBOARD. There was also a place to drop and swap junk that could be reused by someone else.

"Welcome to the grand opening of the SpongeBob SquarePants Recycling Center!" said Sandy.

The crowd cheered and applauded.

THE SPONGEBOB SQUAREPANTS RECYCLING CENTER

JUNK SWAP

PAPER·CARDBOARD

ALUMINUM

GLASS·PLASTIC

"But, Sandy," said SpongeBob. "I already *have* a recycling center."

"I know," said Sandy. "But this one will be run by the city of Bikini Bottom. I told the folks at city hall about your recycling project and they loved it. Now you only have to recycle your own stuff—and you can go back to your job at the Krusty Krab!"

SpongeBob thought for a moment.

"No more endless days of sorting junk in the blazing hot sun?" asked SpongeBob.

"That's right!" said Sandy. "And if everyone recycles, all those innocent sea critters will be safer *and* Bikini Bottom will look more beautiful than ever!"

"That's great!" SpongeBob cheered. "See, Squidward? I told you my junk would be worth something someday!"

THE SPONGEBOB SQUAREPANTS RECYCLING CENTER

"The city would also like to present you with this Green Medal of Honor," Sandy said, putting the medal around SpongeBob's neck.

"Wow," said SpongeBob. "Hey, Sandy, what does 'green' mean?"

"Green means you do your part to keep the world beautiful and healthy," said Sandy.

"Then you can call me Mister GreenPants!" cried SpongeBob.

Then SpongeBob thought for a moment. "Sandy, I wish everyone were green," he added.

"You said it, little buddy," said Sandy. "I sure wish that too."